THIS WALKER BOOK BELONGS TO:

1
2
3
4
5

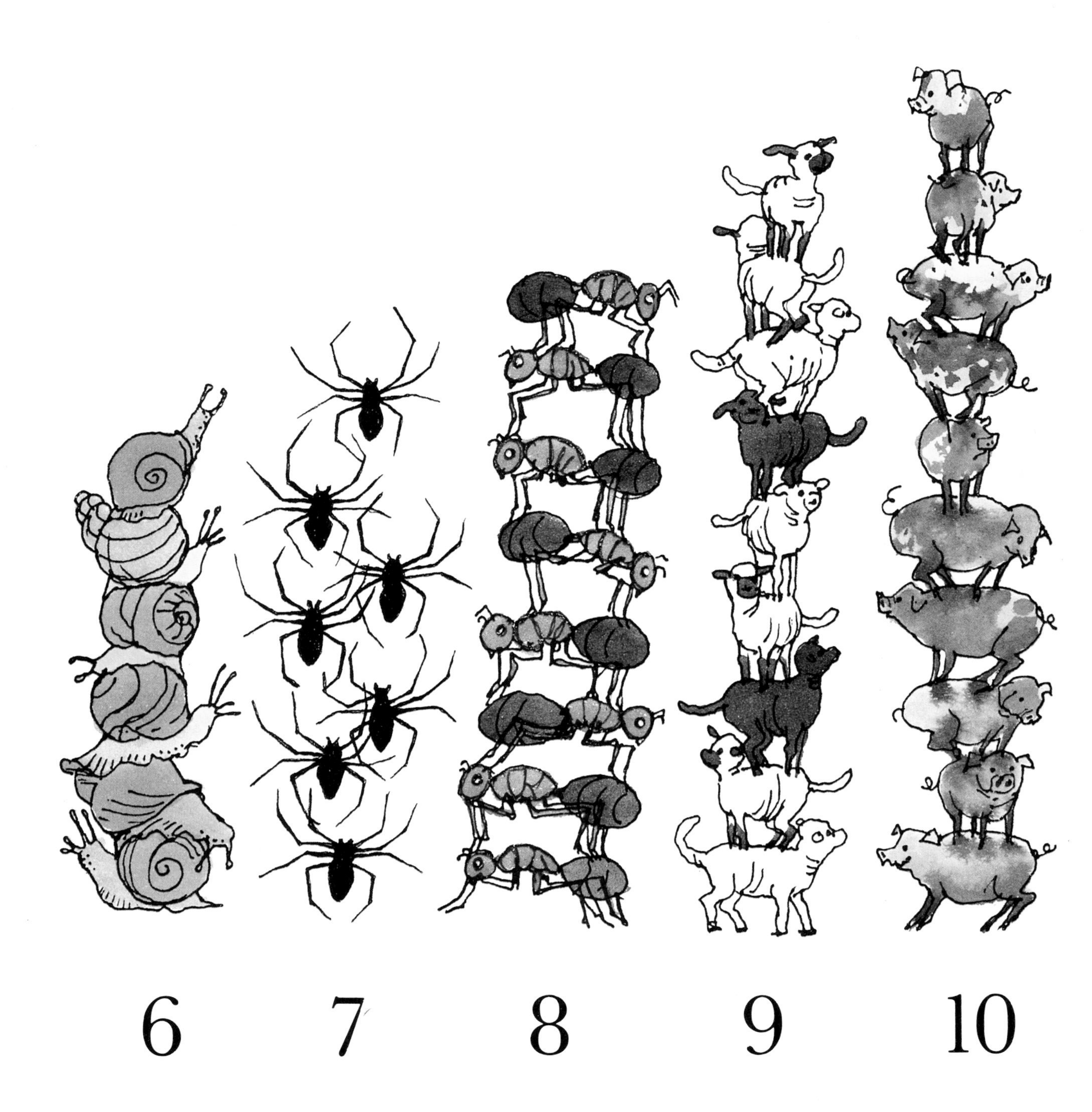
6
7
8
9
10

First published 1986 by Walker Books Ltd
87 Vauxhall Walk, London SE11 5HJ
as *Young Joe*

This edition published 1990

Printed in Italy by Graphicom srl

British Library Cataloguing in Publication Data
Ormerod, Jan
Joe can count.
I. Title
823'.914[J] PZ7
ISBN 0-7445-1343-X

Joe Can Count

Jan Ormerod

WALKER BOOKS
LONDON

1

Joe can count
one fish,

2

two frogs,

3

three mice,

4

four chicks,

five turtles,

6

and six snails.

7

Joe can count
seven spiders,

8

eight ants,

9

nine little lambs,

4
5
6
7
8
9

10

and
ten playful piglets.

5
6
7
8
9
10

Joe can count
one, two,
three, four,

five, six, seven,
eight, nine,
ten little puppies . . .

and one puppy
chooses Joe
for its very own!

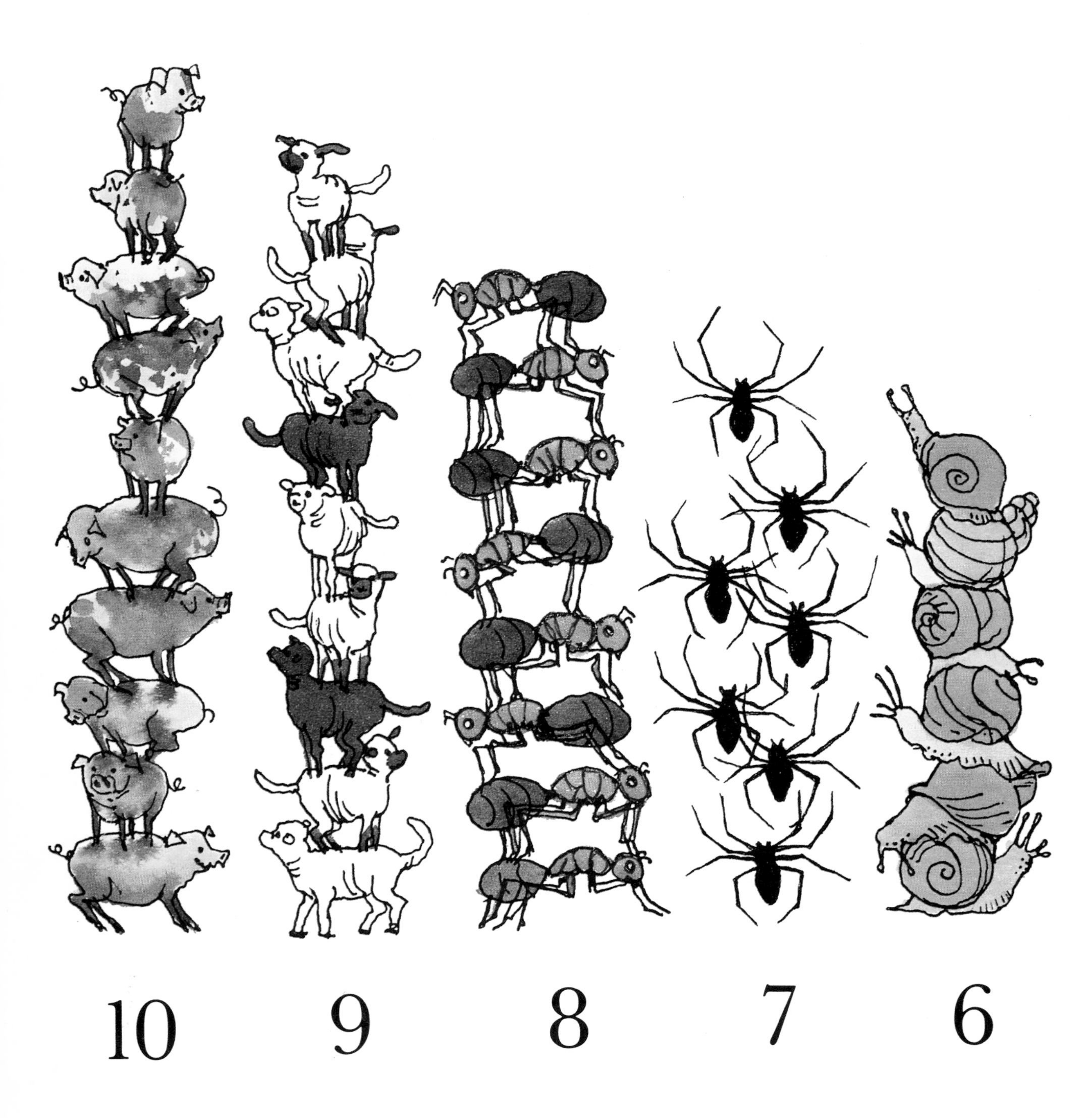
10
9
8
7
6

5
4
3
2
1

MORE WALKER PAPERBACKS

THE PRE-SCHOOL YEARS

John Satchwell & Katy Sleight

Monster Maths

ODD ONE OUT BIG AND LITTLE
COUNTING SHAPES ADD ONE SORTING
WHAT TIME IS IT? TAKE AWAY ONE

FOR THE VERY YOUNG

John Burningham

Concept books

COLOURS ALPHABET
OPPOSITES NUMBERS

Byron Barton

TRAINS TRUCKS BOATS AEROPLANES

PICTURE BOOKS

For All Ages

Colin McNaughton

THERE'S AN AWFUL LOT OF WEIRDOS IN OUR NEIGHBOURHOOD
SANTA CLAUS IS SUPERMAN

Russell Hoban & Colin McNaughton

The Hungry Three

THEY CAME FROM AARGH!
THE GREAT FRUIT GUM ROBBERY

Jill Murphy

FIVE MINUTES' PEACE
ALL IN ONE PIECE

Bob Graham

THE RED WOOLLEN BLANKET
HAS ANYONE HERE SEEN WILLIAM?

Philippa Pearce & John Lawrence

EMILY'S OWN ELEPHANT

David Lloyd & Charlotte Voake

THE RIDICULOUS STORY OF GAMMER GURTON'S NEEDLE

Nicola Bayley

Copycats

SPIDER CAT PARROT CAT CRAB CAT
POLAR BEAR CAT ELEPHANT CAT

Peter Dallas-Smith & Peter Cross

TROUBLE FOR TRUMPETS

Philippe Dupasquier

THE GREAT ESCAPE

Sally Scott

THE THREE WONDERFUL BEGGARS

Bamber Gascoigne & Joseph Wright

AMAZING FACTS BOOKS 1 & 2

Martin Handford

WHERE'S WALLY?
WHERE'S WALLY NOW?